A CITY OF DEVILS

By
Nils Grevillius

Illustrated by
Bruce Litz

Cover Art By
Bruce Litz and Eddie Segura

Edited By
Holly Clearman

Produced by
Laughing Cow Media

September 2013

ISBN-13: 978-1492311539
ISBN-10: 1492311537

Dedicated to the memory of
Joseph Eugene Ferris
who once instructed,
"If you love anything enough,
it shall surrender every secret to you."

Tuesday, 6:15 pm

I'd worked late, or later than usual, arriving at my favorite watering hole, Harry's Club 120, in Old Town. Time for a pop. Harry was behind the bar, sleeves rolled up to reveal inky green skull-n-bones on a muscular bicep. At first blush, some might take Harry Rabbani for an ex-con. I knew better. Besides owning the joint, he was my good, if somewhat older friend, and a reliable confidant.

Confidants, like confidence and confidentiality, are the cornerstones of the business, so they say. Sounds good anyway.

I was annoyed to see Alan Shivers parked at my stool at the bar…all six feet six inches of him, hunched over the bar like a praying mantis, sucking on what was probably the sixth beer of the evening, purchased on an over extended tab. It's my stool, because I'm there so often, and because it's in the corner. I can watch what's going on in front of me without worrying about what's going on behind me.

I grabbed Shiv in a Vulcan Nerve Pinch and guided him over three stools to the left…far enough away that I wouldn't have to listen to his constant mumbling and so I wouldn't have to police my change on the bar. Shiv was a thief as well as a mooch.

Harry was pouring me a draft of golden suds when Shiv piped up, louder than usual, "Real sorry to hear about Ritchey, Fitz…real sorry." I took a drink, not knowing what Shiv was talking about. Shiv was looking at me sideways, as though he expected an answer.

"Okay, I'll bite, Shiv…what gives with Ritchey?" I asked, knowing he was speaking of my former field agent.

"You know, Fitz…that thing with him in Sierra Grove and all…" Shiv was still looking at me funny.

"Shiv, quit fucking around and tell me what you're talking about."

"Well, shit, Fitz, I was sure youda heard by now…Ritchey was found dead in a motel over in Sierra Grove. Hell, musta been Saturday night or so."

"Where'd you hear that?" I asked, taking another pull on the suds.

"Was up in the Grove doin' some banking and I read about it in that little dog-shit newspaper they publish up there." Harry was wiping the glasses dry with the tail of his apron, looking at Shiv.

"News to me Shiv…" I knew it was true; it had to be. But I wouldn't be convinced until I talked to the Medical Examiner. Shiv was a crook and bad check artist, but he knew better than to pull my leg.

I dismissed the thought and asked Harry if any mail had arrived for me. Yeah, I have an office, and an apartment, but I do get

some mail, important mail, at the Club 120.
I make phone calls there too. Harry handed
me a couple of envelopes. One was a letter
from the Chamber of Commerce, asking me to
join. I handed it back to Harry, who filed
it in the garbage can behind the bar without
asking. The other was addressed to me in
care of the Club 120 in Ritchey's uneducated
scrawl. I caught the Shiv trying to read
over my shoulder. Did I mention he was
obnoxious? "Hose off, ass-eyes…" as I
pocketed the letter.

That Ritchey was found stiff in a motel room
didn't surprise me. He was always shacked
in some cheap joint, a week at a time,
usually with a whore, either professional or
amateur, taking life low.

I had another beer, and when Shiv went to the
john, I motioned Harry over. "You heard
anything about Ritchey?"

"Just what Shiv said, Luke." Harry had his
palms turned up. "But it sounds like Ritchey,
motel and that…"

"Yeah, Harry, I know…"
Ritchey had worked for me off and on for ten
years. I met him not too long after I left
Pinkerton's. Short, Italian, and from
somewhere in the East, Ritchey showed up in
my office with some chicken shit resume he'd
pecked out on a library typewriter. It was
his lucky day. I was shorthanded with too
much to do and not enough legs.

He'd graduated from one of those cheesy
correspondence courses you see advertised in

the back of men's magazines: "Be a private detective…and earn big money…" Sure, big money.

I gave Ritchey some leg work that day, and he agreed to a small hourly rate. He got the work done, which while not especially difficult, he'd done it the way I specified. As a test, I gave him a subpoena to serve at an address I knew was bogus.

Came back the next day, "Mr. Fitz, that deponent's address was a mail drop."

"No shit?"

Ritchey got more work, and did it all well, but he had one fault I noticed from jump. He was too slow getting to the office when I paged him. I timed him…two hours to get in. Bracing him I asked, "Renzullo, your motel is in Hollywood. That's twelve miles from here. Why's it take you so long to get here?"

He scraped and looked around the room and was about the change the subject but knew better. "Well, Mr. Fitz, it's 'cause I'm riding the bus, and it takes too long, you know?"

I'd had plenty of field agents, some good, others not. Never had I known one to ride the bus. Hell, they all had cars and weren't as good as Ritchey. I bought him a car, a beater that Harry was selling. I was money ahead.

Surveillance, background checks, court research, telephone gags, Ritchey could do it all. If he had any weaknesses, it was booze

and gambling. Degenerate gambler he was...the
ponies, college basketball, pro football,
Vegas, pai gow at the rummy card joints the
Viets run in the smaller towns along the
freeways. Couldn't drink, but did it anyway.
Couldn't stand to be flush, hated success.
Always in debt or in dutch with a woman over
something. I'd never known the guy to have
the same telephone number longer than a
month. A moving target is harder to hit.
Booze and bookies caused us to part ways,
Ritchey and me.

When it comes to boozing, I have a few now and
again…maybe every night. Probably too much,
but not on the job.

Ritchey couldn't help himself. The gambling
goes without saying. I figure I've got the
whole works at risk every day...why would I
gamble?

Sometimes he'd make shit up to cover himself
and it caused problems. I'm in the facts and
details business. Ritchey didn't want to do
anything about it, and I couldn't do it for
him. It wasn't like I fired him; he just
didn't show up anymore, and I didn't call
him. He fired me and I fired him.

10:45 pm

I hoisted the tail end of my eighth, and
maybe last brew, walked to the other end of
the bar, pulled the jukebox out from the
wall, unplugged it in mid Hank Williams, and
locked myself in the phone booth. A drunk
was staggering over to plug the box back in,
cursing, when Harry caught his attention

with a fresh pop. Turning to the phone, I dropped some dimes and called the back line at the Medical Examiner's Office, the number only the cops are supposed to have. It rang three times and was answered by Jose, the ghoul in green scrubs and rubber apron who weighs and measures the incoming customers.

"M.E., hello......." He grumbled.

"Jose…it's Fitz, up in Pasadena. Remember me?" I hedged, hoping he didn't.

"Not really…whaddaya want? I'm kinda busy, ay."

"Did you do triage on a stiff outta the Grove Saturday night….Sunday morning, early like?" He wouldn't remember. They handle 4000 dead folks a year. Jose went into the computer, like I wanted. That's why I called him at the time and place that I did. I needed facts, not bureaucratic bullshit and endless voicemail mazes.

"Yeah. Renzullo, Richard C. We picked him up at the Regal Inn in the Grove about eleven a.m., Sunday last. Knife victim. Someone let the air outta him." Jose giggled. Like most of them do. It's funny, a joke…dead people are.

"Who caught the case?" I had an idea, but I needed it confirmed.

"Slack. Larry Slack, who else? Say…there's a security hold on this jacket…which agency are you with?" Jose the bureaucrat. I hung

the phone up gently. Just then, Hank
Williams started again. The drunk with the
free beer was glaring at me for interrupting
his hillbilly reverie. Fuck him.

I finished my beer and stepped out onto
Colorado Boulevard. A good shopping night.
The sidewalks were busy in front of well
lit storefronts. I saw none of it.

11:05 p.m.

I opened the letter from Ritchie. It was
short and didn't give up much.

Luke:

*I made a pretty good score with a partner I no
longer trust. I might need an escort out of
the Grove, if you know what I mean. Grove
P.D. has all of the motel phones tapped one
way or another, otherwise I'd call. I am
moving to the Tropic Palms in half an hour. I
have a new old lady. You'll probably like her.
Call me at the Palms as soon as you get this.*

R.R.

Wednesday, 9:30 am

I drove in late rush hour traffic to the
County Recorder's Office in Norwalk, a
crummy suburb in the San Gabriel Valley.
There was a security hold on Ritchey's file.
I wasn't going to get anything from
Detective Larry Slack 'cept a hard way to
go, at least not till I had some facts
independently. Then I'd give the crookedest
detective in the crookedest town in the

county a chance to lie to me.

The line for death certificates was long and there was, of course, a form to be filled out and a fee to be paid. Then you're supposed to wait two months for the clerks to get their shit together and mail you a copy of the certificate. I weathered the line which I shared with mothers carrying all manner of young children. The sun was shining through the glass. I wished I'd brought my sunglasses in from my car. When I got the head of the line, I had my form and check ready. I slid the whole thing through the slot in the bottom of the window along with a folded double sawbuck. The clerk didn't blink, but rather took the form and the check, rang the transaction up, palmed the $20 bill, and proceeded to print out the death certificate.

I studied him as it was printing, having tired of the screaming children and cacophony of languages present in most county offices. He was your typical county clerk: 35 to 50 years old, wearing a nondescript art print necktie and a cheap shirt, pack of Salems in the pocket, looking as though he might turn to putty if he moved any slower.

"Have a nice day, Mr. Fitz." He handed me the envelope with the certificate and a receipt for the check. It's not bribery; it's asshole tax. I pay asshole tax so I can get information in time to work with it.

Strolling across the parking lot, I skinned the certificate out of the envelope. It listed cause of death as "exsanguination as the result of numerous wounds by a sharp instrument." In other words, someone stabbed Ritchey Renzullo enough times that he bled to death. No shit. I perused the certificate further. It listed as reporting party and next of kin a "Mercy Peralta, girlfriend." Never heard of Mercy Peralta, but I wasn't surprised by that.

12:10 p.m.

The Regal Inn was right on Grove Boulevard, the main and only drag in Sierra Grove. It had faded signage with half of the bulbs burnt out. It looked like it was a non-stop crime scene…I could make a felony case in any room, on any day of any week. First Class shit-hole. They shoulda put a sign up advertising rooms by the hour. That's the kind of motel it was. In a reputable town, they'd shut the Regal Inn down, but not in the Grove.

The proprietor appeared to be Chinese, not too long off the boat. He had a crock pot going on the back counter and was watching TV at triple the volume a sane person can stand. Plastic palms with cigarettes smushed out in the pots artlessly decorated the grim lobby. A busted soda machine's neon sign blinked on and off, changing the lighting second by second.

As I approached the counter, he shoved a registration card across the counter at me, never taking his eyes from the TV. I shoved it back to him, opening my wallet to show him my credentials. I didn't know or care if he read them. "I'm looking for Mercy

Peralta."

The motelier looked up. "Not here no
more...never again I not rent to her!"
"Whyzat?"

"She don't pay the rent...have party, some
police problem, you know..." He was nervous.

"Yeah? How long didya rent to Ritchey
Renzullo?" I was onto something.

"A week, two weeks maybe...I 'ready told
Detective Slack...what do you want?" They
get bold when they've paid enough
mordida...start thinking they have rights,
shit like that.

"Were they sharing a room, Mercy 'n Renzullo?"
I ignored his question.

"Sometimes his room, sometimes hers...not for
more than one week...county ordinance!" The
county had ruled that no one could stay in
the same motel for more than a week.
Supposed to discourage dereliction, or
something like that. Vice and parole agents
seemed to like it more than anyone else.
Keeps the riff-raff on the move.

"Where'd she go? Mercy, I mean." The
frustrated Asian pointed cross the street
to his competition, the Tropic Palms Motel.
He described Mercy as Hispanic, short, with
braided hair, always in jeans and a tee-
shirt.

I crossed the street. Tropic Palms was every
bit as high quality as the Fleagal Inn,

except it was under the ownership of an East Indian with wild grey hair and skin as dark as tar paper. He was somewhat less intransigent than his colleague across the street, directing me to room 222. The stairwell reeked of barf and urine, while the hallway was fresher. It smelled like fried food.

I reached Room 222, on the second floor, naturally, and as I went to knock at the door, I could hear someone talking loud, on a telephone, I guessed, and the sound of shitty disco music playing on a radio or boom box. I knocked. I knocked again. I heard a woman's voice say "I got a trick...gotta go."

The door was thrown open by a tall woman sporting a shock of red-blonde hair. Unnatural was the color. A black stretch top, too much tits in evidence. Sometimes less is more. Green eye shadow. Thick, cloying, sweet perfume washed over me. I pitied in an instant anyone patronizing this, knowing that the perfume was being used to cover the stench of an unwashed body. This couldn't be Mercy Peralta.

"You Mercy?" I asked as coyly as could be expected.

"I am if you want me to be." Nothing sexy about it. More tentative...the eyebrows going up. "Who wants to know?"

I flipped my wallet open so she could read the creds, closing them before she could. "I need to talk to her."

"Yes, but, who are you? Larry Slack is working that case." I could tell she was someone I needed to talk to.
"I'm a PI, name's Fitz. Did you know Ritchey?"

"Yeah, I knew Ritchey, but not that well. I'm kinda new in town." She was batting her eyes. "Why's a PI involved....insurance money?"
"Something like that. What's your name?" I put it back on her.

"Lisa. Are you looking for Mercy?"

"That's what I said. Is she around?"

"No need to get shitty, dick." She was a smart ass. She had also already talked to Slack...that much was apparent.

I was going to start in again when Lisa interrupted me. "Detective Slack is looking for Mercy also...so am I."

"Okey. I know why Slack wants her. What's your game?" Lisa's perfume was overwhelming.

"She owes me some money." Her eyebrows were arched for emphasis. A typical whore, Lisa knew how she looked from every angle.

"So why are you in here? Shouldn't you be looking for her?"

Lisa considered my questions. Not smart; crafty. She was cooking up a good lie.

Whores love to lie, but they make great informants. Just ask any Vice Cop. Lousy witnesses but great informants.
"Gotta earn a living, dick."

"Your pimp going to get mad, you talkin' to me? You know I'm not giving up a nickel, at least not until you give up a little something."

"Oh, do you like what you see?" She had whipped a saggy, speckled tit with a jailhouse tat of a palm tree from her spaghetti strap top. "Dick, I don't have a pimp...I'm independent."

"That's not what I meant, Lisa...where the fuck is Mercy?" She put her tit away.

Damn. "Might be we could make a deal, dick. You wanna work for me?"

"You can't afford me. 'sides, I'm not going to find her unless you give me a little help."

She didn't like that. "Dick, I'm a popular ass ho...men like me...y'understand?"

I ignored the puffery. "Where's she from? Is she a pro? Who's her pimp? Or is she freelancing like you?"

"L.A. somewheres. She's as pro as me when she's sprung. Her pimp, last I heard, was Val Bonais." Lisa had produced a nail file like they all do and was whittling away at a nail as big as a Zulu war shield, similarly painted.

I went to get up, thanking the nice lady when she asked, "Hey, dick, can I be your CI?"

"No thanks, Honey, I got enough of them already."

I watched her as I backed out of the room, closing the door. Down the stairs and through the lobby, I couldn't shake the stench of the cheap perfume. The Indian fixed me with a knowing grin. I didn't bother telling him that I hadn't fucked her. Who could? Ritchey maybe. No doubt the Indian heard it before. My car was in the sun. I rolled all of the windows down and drove around the block three times fast. It still stunk of cheap perfume. That pretty much ate up the day.

5:30 p.m.

I arrived at the Club 120. Nothing fancy...just a bar. Harry had a cold one poured by the time my ass hit the top of the stool. I paused before tasting the suds, taking in the drunks who'd been curing under blue neon all day, and then the drunks coming in for happy hour. Changing of the guard. Shivers must have still been sore from the evening before. He stayed at the other end of the bar, cadging beer and smokes from anyone within range. Fucking thief.

I had half a beer and went over to the juke box. The regulars knew what I was doing when I unplugged it. I got the Sheriff's Vice Unit on the phone. They don't start answering until after 6 p.m.

"San Gabriel Valley Vice. Deputy Underwood. C'n I help you?"

"Yeah it's Fitz up in Pasadena. You got any FIs on a pimp named Bonais? Also one of his girls named Mercy Peralta?"

"Yeah, those are good names. Hang on." Underwood knew me from a few prior capers. I looked out of the phone booth. Harry was showing a taped boxing match on the television. Good man. Buying me some peace and quiet. I usually only make one phone call a night.

"Bonais, yeah he works in the Grove. Goes by the moniker "Bones". We have some old cards on him. Nothing on the girl though."

"What's his physical? His horsepower?" It was a natural that Bonais would work the Grove. As long as he passed street tax along to the right guys, he could work hassle free. If Sierra Grove Police took FIs, I was sure they were used for shake downs.

FIs are field interview cards. Cops filled out FIs when they detained, stopped, buttonholed or jacked anyone up for anything. That is if they were doing their job. They kept them in a big shoebox in the vice office...pimps, hoes, fences, johns, dealers, muggers, perverts, counterfeiters, gypsies.

Underwood, a large black man with a sonorous voice, described Bonais as "a piss yellow Negro" sporting an ugly scar across his face

courtesy of a girl gone bad. He was about
six feet five inches and a buck fifty.
Skinny. Always wearing a twenty years out of
date Members Only jacket and a dew-rag on his
head. Underwood related that his last known
auto was a Buick low-rider with a peeling
vinyl top a la Frito-Lay. Nice.

I rejoined my beer, and had a few more
on top of that.

Thursday, 8:15 a.m.

There was a plain wrap cop car in the alley
next to my office building. Maroon with a
license plate frame reading "Beautiful Sierra
Grove." Slack.

I rode the elevator to the seventh floor,
went into the men's room, climbed out onto
the fire escape at the rear of the building,
and strolled down a half flight. Looking in
the hallway window, I could see the familiar
shape of Detective Larry Slack, ample ass
parked on the bench up the hall from my
office. I ascended the escape, and took the
stairs down, coming up behind Slack.
Calculated to annoy an annoying man.

"Fitz...what are doing creeping around here?"
He put down the Grove Press, the dog-shit
newspaper published by one of the city
fathers up there. Slack had a thick neck and
short legs, like a high school wrestling
coach. His jowls were parked on crushed shirt
collars and concealed what was probably the
sloppiest knot ever put to a neck tie. He
stunk of cigar butts and graft. His pink
sweaty mug was topped off with a mismatched
toupee...must have cost him all of thirty

dollars. Vanity.

"It's my office, Slack. I do business here. What's on your mind?" I unlocked the door and walked in. I had my back to him...didn't want to give him the satisfaction of knowing I didn't trust his sorry ass.

I turned on the lights and motioned for Slack to take a seat. I keep a special chair in my office; low to the floor and comfortable enough to fall asleep in. I'm a tall guy, but from the chair behind my broad expanse of desk, I dominate the room, and thus anyone sitting there. Slack sat for a moment and disliked the arrangement, taking to his feet.

"You been poking around the Grove, Fitz, working one of my cases. Why didn't you call first?" He had a point. Any other department, I'd have done them the courtesy.

"I don't owe you shit, Slack. Why didn't you call me yourself to tell me Ritchey was chilled, huh? Didn't think I'd be interested? You knew Ritchey was like a little brother to me, cocksucker." I wanted him to think I cared more than I did.

"Hey, Luke, let's start over here. You gotta point. Maybe I should have called you first, but you know how it is."

He had his hands on his hips. He was wearing a grey Armani suit but with his weird build and hunched posture, he'd ruined it in the space of a morning. I didn't say anything.

I wanted him to do the talking. I knew what was next.

"Say, Fitz, you don't mind accounting for your whereabouts Saturday night, Sunday morning, do ya?" He was grinning. That was supposed to make me nervous.

"Club 120 and my apartment, 429 North Euclid. I thought you wanted to start over." Slack sat down again.

"Can anyone verify that?" He was blowing smoke, buying time. He had something else on his mind.

"Harry Rabbani and my landlady, Tess Johnson. 'sat all?"

"Yeah, I hear you're rousting legit businessmen over in the Grove. We don't 'zactly appreciate that, Fitz."

"Which ones? The whores? The pimps? Maybe the fences? The bookies? Oh, hell, I forgot. You plumb ran every goddamned bookie outta town." I was hissing and grinning at him. "I got a license from the State saying I can go into any city from San Diego to the Oregon border, ask any kind of questions I like of any motherfucker I meet." He didn't like it, but hung in. He wasn't done.

"Your license doesn't mean shit in the Grove, Fitz." Quite matter-of-factly, he meant it.

"Naw, Fitz, those motel guys. They're a big source of city revenue." Yeah and shake down money. It went without me saying it.

"Fitz, I gotta know if you got any information on this here murder. I know Ritchey was your pal and alla that, but this is an ongoing investigation. I'm gonna clear this case." It was no secret that while the Grove didn't have the highest murder rate in the county, they had the highest unsolved rate, thanks to Slack and his cohorts.

"I don't know shit about it, Slack, and if I did, it would be presented to the D.A. You couldn't find a burglar in a motherfucking phone booth."

"Fitz, I'm warning you...if you're holding out on me, I'll beef you for obstructing justice." Slack took to his feet again.

"Book me or get the fuck out of here." I was on my feet too. Not as mad as he thought I was. "I've got criminals to catch, and I might catch you."

He stalked out. It was too easy. I was surprised he didn't ask me anymore. A half hour of softballs. He wasn't working the case. He was working an angle. And what was I doing? Trying to find out who killed a friend. Ritchey would have done the same for me, I hoped.

I walked into the hallway and spotted Slack's plain wrap round the corner, cigar smoke puffing out the driver's window. I stole back to my office and pulled the cushion out of the chair. His badge wallet. Asshole had left his badge, with ID, under the cushion. Didn't matter if he'd done it intentionally or on accident. He'd be back. If it was on purpose, he had another and could risk losing one. If it was an accident, I could have some fun with it. Either way, I needed to unass the office. Grabbing my jacket, I tucked an eight ounce beavertail sap into my waistband. It was going to be one of those days.

11:20 a.m.

There was work to be done on paying cases, running leads at the United States Criminal Courts downtown. I dropped Slack's badge into the U.S. Mail collection box in front of the Federal Building. Maybe the Postal Inspector would take a hint and open a case on Larry Slack. Maybe they already had.
1:45 p.m.

I took lunch, liquid naturally, at a joint in Chinatown. It had a big fancy neon sign, called itself "Quon Yin Temple." Fancy name for a dive bar frequented by cops. I was napping in the corner booth when my pager went off. It was Harry.

I dropped a couple of dimes in the slot of the payphone. Harry answered on the first ring, "Fitz, that you?"

"It's me. What's shaking?"

"Judge Haagebach's clerk just called. Larry Slack is over trying to get a search warrant for your office...something about heisted police equipment." Harry was a little agitated.

"Is that so?" That was the game.

"Yeah, Luke. Are you okay?"

"Got it under control. Do me a favor. Call Frank Gallo. Tell him to get over to Haagebach's chambers. Get a copy of asshole's affidavit for search. Tell him to stipulate to a consensual search only in his presence."

"Whose presence, Luke?"

"Gallo's presence, Harry. He's my attorney, remember?"

"Got it." He rang off. Harry was strictly old school. A loyal friend.

Slack's game was plain as day. He'd come by looking to hose me for information and when I wasn't giving it up, planted his badge in the office. I couldn't wait to read his affidavit. He'd have to lie like a whore to get a warrant out of an old gent like Judge Haagebach. There was no way he'd put up with the humiliation of having to search the shop in front of my lawyer and with the stip, Haagebach wouldn't likely sign a warrant.

6:55 pm

Harry was at the front door of the Club 120
ejecting Alan Shivers. Something about
stealing money off of the bar. He'd be back.
Harry's a nice guy. Besides, Shiv had a tab
to pay.

I sat down at my stool and Harry handed me
a manila envelope. He poured me a draught
while I opened the envelope. On top was
Gallo's bill. He's a lawyer, what else
would he do? Underneath that was Slack's
affidavit.

"Withholding evidence...concealing stolen

police property...interfering in an
official investigation…" Baked air.
The note from Gallo stated in part that
Slack had tried to withdraw the search
warrant request upon Gallo's arrival. I was
sure he wasn't exaggerating. Judge
Haagebach wouldn't permit it, instead
denying the request and keeping the
affidavit that Slack wanted back. Actually,
I think the crooked detective wanted the
crime report back. He had, as most homicide
cops do, attached the crime report to the
request and affidavit as an exhibit.
Hearsay though it may be, crime reports have
an impact. This one was a doozy.

The usual forced outline, black ballpoint on
white forms. I nearly wept when I read that
Ritchey had been stabbed better than thirty
two times. All puncture wounds with an ice
pick found at the scene. He'd been bound and
gagged. Tortured. Someone wanted something
from him other than just his life.

The report was signed by M.X. Carmody of the
Sierra Grove PD. An old harness bull, I'd
known Carmody for years. He hadn't called
me either. The witness included a white
female named Lisa Carpenter with date of
birth and driver's license number. Her
horsepower jibed with the whore I'd
interviewed at the Tropic Palms. She listed
her occupation as "entertainer." Oh yeah.

Lisa, as far the crime report went, stated
that she'd returned to the Regal Inn at 4
a.m. and had a key, having been given one
earlier the preceding evening by decedent
Richard Renzullo. She found him tied to a

chair in the motel room, gagged and dead.
Called the cops a half hour later. Edwin
Zhou, proprietor of the Regal Inn, was the
only other witness listed. He verified
Ritchey's rental of the room and provided a
copy of the registration card which was
xeroxed and attached to the report.

I had another draught. Then another. Then, I
had two fingers of Bushmills, neat. With a
water back. Thirty two times, with an ice
pick. Someone wanted to really hurt
him, really hated him. Ex cons like ice
picks. It's a legit tool for the household,
you can't get beefed by your parole agent,
unless of course you're carrying it on your
person. It is also deadly. The whiskey went
down slow, setting my chest on fire. I needed
it.

Contemplating Slack's affidavit and crime
report, there was something missing. I
didn't know what. Slack wanted to search my
office. He was looking for Mercy Peralta.
Lisa Carpenter had told me that. It was a
safe bet that whatever she'd told me about
Mercy, she'd laid off on Slack and then some.
It was obvious that she was one of Slack's
confidential informants. She as much as
called herself one. But was she truthful? If
she was looking for Mercy as well, she'd
nothing to lose. That was what was wrong
with the report. Slack didn't log a single
entry to the report until after my interview
of Carpenter the preceding day. Three days
had passed without asshole lifting a finger.

I had to get with Bonais, the piss colored
Negro, if I was going to authenticate any of

Lisa Carpenter's story.

11:35 p.m.

I'd paced myself. Not too much booze.
Especially not whiskey. I exited the freeway
at Grove Boulevard and headed south. The
Grove at night was a jungle of titty bars,
saloons, and small casinos disguised as
fraternal lodges. Motels too, always located
close to fast food stands, gas stations and
the stop-n-rob convenience stores that litter
the San Gabriel Valley. Aesthetically, hours
of darkness were no kinder to the Grove than
sunlight was. It just revealed something
different about the place. It brought out the
skells, whores, dealers and trash that
dominate the kind of places I was going to.

Driving the boulevard twice, I hadn't made
the Buick low rider that Bones was supposed
to be driving. Spotting a whore on her
track in front of a boarded up market, I
pulled to the curb. She got closer and I
could see that she was Latin, 22 going on
dead, dirty feet and no front teeth.

"You want to party, ay?" She asked. Not
especially, I thought.

She was slathered in Lisa's brand of
perfume...Eau de Ho? I laid a fin on her
before she could get in the car. She told
me that Bones held court in a pool hall at
Grove and Tropic. I thanked her and
motored.

I drove around the pool hall twice. It was in
the corner of a strip mall, parking lot out
front with a few cars, not the Buick. I made
the Buick in the alley behind the place,
parked alongside the cars of the other
regulars. The front lot was for rubes and
suckers. Too easy for the rollers to
make you if you're in plain sight.

Eyeballing the place, I mulled over my
approach. Wait for him to come out? Go in
and jack him. I took the sap from my waist,
and put the strap around my hand. It wasn't
like the movies. The music didn't stop nor
did the chatter of the skells. I didn't see
any of my friends in the place. I looked
around the dimly lit room, lamp hanging low
over green felt, dance music, the clacking
of pool balls. Over to my right, I made out
Bones chalking up a cue stick, dew rag on
his head, shirtsleeves above bony elbows,

forearms covered with jailhouse ink. It
contrasted nicely with his piss yellow
complexion.

I ignored Bones, went to the bar. The
bartender, a one armed former liquor
store bandit named Cisco, got me a beer.

"It's on me, Fitz."

Hoisting the beer with my left, I kept the
sap ready in my right hand along my
trouser leg. I didn't think he remembered
me. Ambling back to the vicinity of the
table where Bones was shooting 8-Ball, I
took the measure of the place. Seven pool
tables, a shuffleboard table, two dart
boards, about fifty customers. I wondered
how many of them were narcs or parole
agents.

Stepping over, I could see that Bones was
about to take his last shot on the 8-ball,
calling it for the corner pocket. He had his
back to me. The ball sank and two birds
leaning against the wall made their move for
the next game. I brushed their change onto
the floor. One of them growled, moving with
his hands out to fight. I brought the sap
down on his shoulder. He buckled at the
knees, pain clouding his pocked face. His
buddy moved in for a taste. Bones waived him
off.

"Rack 'em, dick." He said, chalking up his
cue stick again. "I'll give you as much
time as it takes me to whip yo' ass at this
here pool game, hear?" He had a gulf coast
accent and despite his size, moved around

the table fast. I didn't let him get close
to me. His friends skulked over to the
other end of the room.

"What's on your mind, dick?" he said as he
broke the balls I had racked. I pocketed
the sap, selected a cue stick that didn't
seem too bent, and chalked it.

"Lookin' for one of your girls, Bones." His
first stroke of the stick sank two balls,
both solids. He shot again and missed.

"Yeah? Which one?"

"Mercy." I said as I sank the 9-ball in a
side pocket.

"Don't have no bitches name Mercy workin'
for me, dick." I moved around the table,
watching Bones, watching out for his
friends. I took a pull on my beer and moved
to the other side of the table to shoot at
the 11-ball.

"Not what I heard, Bones." I missed the
shot. He moved in for his, calling it in
the corner pocket. I could see he was
looking to his friends on the other side of
the room. They looked back.

"Told you, dick...I don't have no ho named
Mercy workin' for me. Y'understand? Jes'
like I told that fat dick work fo' the Grove.
Tired of y'all comin' in here fuckin' with
me." He made his next two shots quickly, and
was down to the 8-ball.

"Listen up, ass-eyes. I got someone tellin' me

different. If you want to play fuck-fuck with me, I can make life real fuckin' interesting for you."

He glared at me and took his last shot, saying "Not in the Grove, dick. Not in the Grove you cain't." The 8-ball sank.

"Now, unless you got something to book me on, get the fuck outta my face, dick." He was someone's boy, maybe Slack's but not likely. Probably one of his esteemed colleagues in the Vice Bureau.

I downed my beer and smiled at the piss yellow pimp. "You and I are just getting going, shithead. I'll see you real soon."

My back close to the wall and my sap in my hand, I edged out the back door of the pool hall and into the night. When I got to the end of the alley, I could see that my car door was open. Someone was bent over in the driver's seat. I altered my steps so as to make no sound and closed the distance fast.

As I cleared the end of a dumpster in my approach, I saw in my periphery someone short, thick and fast moving in faster from my left. He pinned my left and had me falling on my right before I could bring the sap up. I hit the ground hard. I looked to my left just in time to catch an incoming view of a fist. Behind the fist was the grinning face of Larry Slack.

I am always surprised by how hard a punch a
guy with short arms can throw. It's like
there's nothing to delay the thought of
hitting you with the connection of the punch.
He had something in his hand, like a roll of
nickels. I went out, my head burning with
pain, choking on my own vomit.

Friday, 4:15 a.m.

The drunk tank in the Grove City Jail is a
choice place to slowly become aware of your
own aching consciousness. I was propped
against the wall, sitting in wet pants. Had
I pissed myself? I didn't care.

There were two metal bunks bolted to the wall
and floor, each occupied by a groggy
sportsman of one description or another. I
was grateful that I couldn't breathe through

my nose, broken again, as the floor was awash
in expectorate, vomit, and excrement. Nice,
really nice. Why didn't I go to dental
school like my little brother?

Not liking what I saw, I went back to sleep.
One at a time, my cell mates made bail or
were kicked loose. I took to a bunk with a
plastic wrapped mattress.

8:30 a.m.

Frank Gallo showed up with one of the Repetti
Brothers bail bondsmen. Fifty grand and
seven signatures later, I was riding in the
back seat of Repetti's car, a nice import.
If he didn't like the way I smelled, he
didn't let on.

"The cops impounded your car, Fitz. Evidence
or something. They say you assaulted a police
officer." He looked up in the rearview
mirror. Gallo said nothing.

"Yeah, I always do that...can't stand the
motherfuckers."

"Luke, this is serious business. Serious
charges," Gallo piped up.

"I know, Frank, but it isn't like what
they're saying. I was working a case,
exited a dive bar, and caught someone
creeping my car. Slack blind-sided me." My
nose was still clogged with blood. I asked
Repetti to take me to a friend's house where
I keep another car.

"Slack's name is nowhere on the report, Luke."

Gallo had turned and was looking at me in the back seat.

"Yeah? Who's the complaining witness?"

"Sianez. Vic Sianez. You know him?"

Sonny Sianez, Vice Detective for the Grove. I knew of him, but had never had the pleasure.

Repetti added, "Ugly guy. Looks like he caught a load of birdshot in each cheek."

The thwarted pool player I'd tamed with my sap. So that's the game. He's Bones' man, or the other way around. They took me to the top of El Molino and dropped me off at Sue's house. I thanked them, weathering my lawyer's admonishment to stay out of the Grove.

Sue is a nice girl, a red head. Artist. Used to be a dancer. Freckles, cheerful, smart. Puts up with me. Might be worthy of her one day. She cleaned me up, washed my clothes, gave me aspirin and put me to her bed. She napped on the couch. I know 'cause I got up to go to the john. She slept with her cat and both dogs around her, trousers undone, phone off of the hook. The sun was setting when I woke.

Her garage is big enough to store my other car, a plain vanilla Volvo sedan. She had jumper cables to help me start it. I let it idle for twenty minutes and took on a little food. Coffee too. She'd seen me worse and didn't lecture me. I knew I couldn't have

more with her unless I mended my ways. She
had already heard from a friend about
Ritchey. Shook her head as I backed the
Volvo out of the driveway.

8:05 p.m.

My conversation with the bondsman gave me an
idea. With the Volvo backed into the alley
onto Garfield Street, I went up to my office
and retrieved a small tool kit. My sap was
gone. I took my belt off enough loops to
thread a holster on, grabbed the four inch
Smith .357 in the lower desk drawer, and
holstered it. Some PIs don't like guns.
Squeamish? Elitist? Who gives a damn? Not
me. I like alla that shit. Saps, guns,
bats...they are all useful at one time or
another. Better to have one and not need
than the other way around. Ritchey was
funny. He could never keep his permit
current. Fail to pay traffic fines and
they'd suspend his driver's license. That
automatically cancelled his permit. Nice
racket the state has going.

He always had his piece when he needed it
though, and that's the rule of thumb I like to
follow: have a gun when you need one.

He and I were working a caper for a jeweler.
We went up to Ventura County to door knock at
the home of a guy who's hung a large rubber
check for a diamond ring. He was supposed to
be a big shot realtor or something like that.
Fairly routine. Knock on the door, ask him
to make good on it. Nothing complicated.
Ritchey had his piece. I left mine in the
car. Just a middle class paper hanger. No

big deal...easy money.

He didn't answer the front door. We went
around to the back to see if his car was
there. Turns out while we're knocking at the
door, he's loading a shotgun. The "realtor"
was an ex-con from Texas who'd jumped bail.
I guess he thought we were there to take him
back. Never got his side of it. Ritchey
dumped him when he came round the side of the
house and stuck the barrels of the sawed off
under my chin. Ritchey settled his hash with
a round in his right eye and another in his
neck. He died before he could kill me. What
a fucking mess. Ruined my shirt. The client
didn't want to pay - we couldn't collect from
a dead man. Clients can be the worst part of
this business.

Yeah, I could count on Ritchey when the
chips were down, just not day to day.
That was too much for him.

Swinging by the Club 120, I checked my mail.
Harry poured me a draught. I couldn't
finish it without my head starting to pound.
Frank Gallo had filled him in on my arrest
the night before. There was a small kitchen
at the Club 120, conditional for Harry
keeping a liquor license.

Pulling some baking soda, lye soap, aspirin
and a crushed urinal cake together, I
mashed it all in a metal mixing bowl with
the head of a mallet. Harry stepped into
the kitchen.

"What're you making, Fitz?" He had a puzzled
look on his face.

"Just making a little crack, Harry. I'll explain later." He looked at me like I'd just bailed out of the state hospital.

"Harry, step down to the head and get me a couple of condoms outta the vending machine, will ya?" He shook his head and went down to the head. I mixed the crushed powders together with some water and Elmer's glue in the bowl and when it was like paste, poured the mess into the skillet on the stove, like a chemical pancake. It hardened quickly.

Finishing my beer, I scraped the hardened mix out of the skillet. Voila! Crack without cocaine. I divvied it up between the two condoms and knotted each.

It was burn. Enough to get you jailed if you tried to sell it, but nothing if you got caught with it. It would take the crime lab a week or two to figure out it wasn't real crack. It looked for all the world like that dispensed in the crummier parts of every city in the country. I had a plan for helping a certain piss yellow Negro make his life right.

9:15 p.m.

More sleep at the Euclid. My home. I'd parked the Volvo two blocks away, just in case, and entered the apartment building from the rear, jumping the fence next to the fig tree so no one could see me. Just in case. Slack wasn't done with me yet. There was no way Bones had given Mercy up to him.

Saturday, 1:00 a.m.

The alarm jolted me awake. My headache brand new again. More aspirin. I brushed my teeth gently because my nose still hurt. When I rinsed my mouth, blood came out. Dark clothes, the holstered gun, and out the back door.

I paused long enough to see if I had a tail. None was in sight. To the Volvo, which almost didn't start. No freeway this time. The Grove had DUI checkpoints at the exits. Perfect for rousting drunks and making more money when they were robbed when being booked by The Grove's finest. Sticking to surface streets, it didn't take much more time to get to the intersection of Grove and Tropic...my favorite pool hall.

The Buick with the Frito-Lay top was docked in the alley. The ball peen hammer from my tool kit took a nice divot out of the tail light. I couldn't chance it there and I needed to find out where the cocksucker stayed anyway, so I waited.

Most businesses turn their lights out when they are closing. Not a saloon or pool hall. They turn them on so the roaches will scurry out into the dark. Even in the Grove, bars close at 2:00 a.m.

Ten minutes after the lights came on, I saw Bones exit the joint, cue stick in a vinyl case under his bony arm. He had his greasy jacket zipped up against the early morning chill. He was comfortable enough to not be looking around, not that he'd have made me as far off as I was.

Bones' Buick roared to life along with the
loud stereo. I could see the motherfucker
ditty-bopping behind the wheel, moving with
the loud dance music blaring from his car.
Following this pile of garbage was going to
be a cinch even without the tail light beacon
I'd made.

I eased out of my curbside observation
post, and keeping it loose, trailed the
pimp seven blocks south on Grove to the 888
Hotel, an SRO. Asshole pulled his car into
a reserved spot in the back. It was nice
and dark as parking lots go. I waited.

The light in a fourth floor room came on,
then the light in the adjoining bathroom
smaller window. Then they both went out.
Time to wait.

3:21 a.m.

Some things can only be done at night under
the cover of darkness, in the wee hours when
people sleep most soundly. Burglary.
Burglars know this; at least the pros do.
So do guys who do "black bag jobs." I stay
away from that kind of action generally, but
this was different.

The slim-jim had Bones' Buick sprung
quickly. Older Detroit iron is always
easier to open. The car reeked of Kool
cigarettes and fast food. I stuffed the
crack filled condoms in the seat cushion
where Bones parked his bony ass. The door
was closed and locked.

I walked back to my own car two blocks away.
I used a round about route just in
case. No one was out. The streetlights
played to an empty house. I rounded the
corner into the alley where the Volvo
was docked. Just ahead was a patrol unit for
Grove P.D. They were probably the only guys
on duty that night. Might have been asleep.
Might have been looking out for me. Not
likely; the Volvo is registered to Harry's
dog. Not worth taking the chance.

Doubling back at the double time, I reach
the 888 Hotel. The lobby was unlocked. A
telephone directory in the doorway. I
found the lone payphone against the wall.
Using the direct dial number rather than
911, I called the Highway Patrol dispatch.

"Nine-One-One...what's your emergency?" A
nasal voice, probably in Sacramento.

"There's a Mexican dude with a gun in the
alley behind the liquor store at Tropic and
Grove." Like a moron.

"In which city, sir?" Annoyed at the caller's
lack of information.

"Sierra Grove, I think." Moron again.

She sighed, "Okay, we'll contact them
directly...stand by."

"Yes ma'am." The phone interrupted, wanting
more change, which I was counting on. The
call disconnected. They'd dispatch it
anyway.

I headed back to my car, approaching the alley from the other direction, just in time to see the Grove coppers pull out with their lights on heading north. Looking for Mexicans with guns. Exciting.

The Volvo pointed south, I headed out of the Grove into county territory and took surface streets to Sue's pad.

The lights were out. The dogs didn't bark when I let myself in. There's a key in a potted plant on the porch. Her bed was warm and so was Sue.

11:17 a.m.

Sue was gone. Coffee was good. The dogs sat, the little one on my lap, the big one on my feet, while I read the paper. I took the day off. Sue and I went for Greek food in Los Angeles then to an art show in Laguna. She likes art. I like her, so the time was well spent. The headache was almost gone but there was still clotted blood coming out of my nose. I had to wear sunglasses to cover up the raccoon eyes that come with every deviation of the septum.

Monday, 8:30 a.m.

I had an appointment with an insurance adjuster. Another paying case. One that wouldn't put me in jail or the hospital. I'd rather work on Ritchey's thing, but I have to pay the bills. Phone calls, answer mail. Have a cup of coffee. A new secretary would be nice. They don't last long. I must be hard to work for.

Gallo's secretary Donna called. The DA declined to file charges on the case for which I'd been booked. She said she was making out my new bill. Terrific.

10:15 a.m.

I called Harry at the Club 120, asked him to shoot over to the Criminal Records counter, run a make for priors on Bonais and Lisa Carpenter. He grumbled a little bit but agreed to get it done as soon as possible. That meant Carmen Rabbani would be tending bar for at least an hour.

He hated it and so did his customers. Nice lady, lousy saloon keeper.

11:49 a.m.

The Planet Club Barbershop. It isn't part of the Planet Club that's associated with the university. Alla the egg-heads hang out over there. The barbershop rents space from them and is open to bums like me.

Joe the barber calls me up to his chair. My turn. Joe's a nice guy. Most bookies are. Never met one I didn't like. His clientele was all of the gentlemen gamblers hanging out at the Planet Club, so most of his action was, naturally, college sports. He was getting pretty far ahead in my haircut when I went to work.

"How's the book, Joe?"

"Pretty good, Fitz...you got anything going?"

"Nothing great. Working a case for a gal, actually."

"What kind of gal, Fitz?" He clipped and talked at the same time.
"Pro, Joe. In over her head with some no-good fucking pimp."

"Any of them any good?" Joe had stopped, and was looking at me in the mirror. Joe was Puerto Rican, from New York, originally. Street smart, but an uncommon polish.

Nodding as best I could in agreement, "I'd like to get him offa the street long enough to get this girl into rehab."

"You got anything on him?" Joe didn't know how much of the hook he had taken.

"Not sure. He is dealing crack, but it's up in the Grove. You know how they always look the other way as long as they get a taste of the green."

"Yeah, I heard about that." Joe used to have a shop in the Grove. Insatiable demand for payoffs from the likes of Slack & co. had driven Joe out.

"Yeah, Joe, this pimp, his name is Bonais. He hangs out at that shitty pool hall..."

"You mean the one at Tropic and Grove?"

"That's the one. Anyway, this pimp, he's

always holding. Keeps his shit in the seat
cushion of his car."

Joe continued cutting my hair silently.
There was a soap opera on. Like a chick, he
watched soap operas every day. I was about to
set the hook again when the barber asked,
"Kind of car does he drive?"

I ran it down to him a bit at time. Joe held
a hand mirror up for me to see my reflection.
Ten bucks is a good price for a haircut these
days, especially if you don't have much to
cut. On my way out, I asked Joe, "Hey. I
gotta work this guy just right. Please don't
mention anything I said about this jamoke to
anyone...okay?"

"You got it Fitz." Telling a bookie to keep
his mouth shut about something was the
surest way to make sure that every cop of
any note in town knew about it multo rapido.
Joe had drawn a bookmaking beef a few years
before in the county area, so I knew he was
with Underwood at the Sheriff's Department.
The only way a bookie can survive the
shakedowns from the outfit and crooked cops
like Slack is to provide information. The
bigger departments protect informants
better.

I crossed the street to the park, loped
around a stand of trees and sat down at a
picnic bench. I could make Joe out on the
telephone in his shop. If I had called
Underwood myself at the Sheriff's Vice
Office, he'd be wondering what kind of angle
I was working. This way was better. Better
for Joe, better for Underwood, and better for

me squeezing the piss yellow pimp. Time for a pop.

1:58 p.m.

Harry and I were alone in the Club 120. Working drunks had gone back to the office or shop. Bonais had a record of felony and misdemeanor prosecution going back to his eighteenth year, anything prior was juvenile records sealed from my prying eyes. He was unable to find any record for Lisa Carpenter as far as a criminal jacket went. Same when he called department of corrections. That was odd. You'd think a piece of shit whore like that would have a jacket for something. Must have been new in town, I thought.

I had a couple of beers. So did Harry. Peach, Harry's bull terrier mix, was stretched out on the floor asleep under the booth. Good idea. Peach was one of those dogs who didn't bark or growl. Just biting was his specialty, kind of like Harry. Peach was an endless source of laughs. People would approach Harry sitting in his booth with the dog and ask "does your dog bite?"

"He sure does." Always the same response. Smart folks kept their distance; idiots cannot.

"But he looks so nice" or some shit like that just before they got their hand trimmed. Hilarious. Peach was the reason Harry had no liability insurance. Good dog.

4:45 p.m.

Just before the evening rush, I barricaded the
phone booth and tried the county jail. Bonais
hadn't been booked yet. A few more beers. I
tried again, still no luck. Drove past the
Euclid. I could swear there was a plain wrap
covering one end of the street.

Roundabout driving got me back to Sue's
place. She asked if I was going to make it a
habit. I told her I didn't know. She put me
on the couch for the night. Nice girl. I
went right to sleep.

Tuesday, 4:05 a.m.

Woke up to piss. Calling the county jail, I
learned that Bones was booked two hours
prior. Narcotics beef. It was time to go to
work. The pimp's bail was set at $100G. He
had, of course, priors. I wanted to get him
out on my terms before Sonny Sianez could
spring him.

I made my own coffee without waking Sue or
her menagerie. The paper wasn't there yet.
He arrived as I was warming the Volvo, a
cup of coffee steaming the windows as it
rested on the dash. News radio predicted
rain. I could see the stars; a cloudless
sky. What the hell did they know?

Repetti met me at his office with a bail
contract and a blank bond to post. He was
half asleep but mentioned that I was
responsible for Bones should he jump bail.
I didn't think it would come to that.

My regular car was in Repetti's lot behind
the office. He'd gotten it out of impound for

me when the DA declined to prosecute. Slack
had tossed it pretty good. The radio was on
the front seat. I docked the Volvo, leaving
half a cup of by then cold coffee on the
dash. I'd be back. County jail was fifteen
minutes down an empty freeway to Bauchett
Street

5:30 a.m.

I waited at inmate reception for Bones to
be brought out. He came out wearing
sneakers with no laces and his head
was nappy for lack of the usual dew rag.
Bones looked like a boiled rooster.

Crossing the parking lot to my car, I was
explaining our new relationship to Bones.
"Your ass is mine. I own you like you own
your hoes. We clear?" He had his back to me
and was half a pace ahead.

"Ain't gonna be all of that. Who dotted
your eyes, dick?" was as much as he got out
before I whacked him behind the ear with my
revolver. He went to his knees, howling
piteously.

"Get up, dipshit. Sonny sold you to me.
You work for Fitz now, asshole." I stood
over him...I'd whack him as many times as
it took. He sensed that. His hands went
up in defeat.

I took him to the all night diner across from
the jail. He cleaned up in the bathroom, had
some coffee and a donut. Started to dance to
my tune. Amazing what half a night in stir
and a pistol whipping can do for a man's

attitude.

"Where's Mercy Peralta." I had no time
to fuck around.

"Man, I wish I knew. Actually, I'm glad I
don't." He snuffled, slurping coffee with too
much sugar. Too much cream. Coffee dribbled
down a bewhiskered chin.

"Whyzat?"

"Everyone is looking for her. Slack, you,
some other ho. 'Smatter of fact, Sonny told me
not to say shit to Slack about her. Know what
I'm saying? Don't they supposed to work
together?"

Not in the Grove. Everyone is in business
for himself. Corruption is king. Bones ran it
down to me. Mercy was Salvadoran from the
Westlake District of L.A. Her dad and
brothers were movers in a street gang combo
whose initials were spray painted over half
of Los Angeles. Mercy only came to the Grove
when she was high. Crack. Her family, even
though they traded in it, wanted her clean
and away from it. Once her money ran out,
she was turned out, first by others, later by
Bones. A real entrepreneur.

"When's the last time you saw her?"

"She has an old man, or did up until a couple
of weeks ago. 'Talian guy named Ritchey."

"Is that the guy killed at the Regal Inn?
What gives with that?" I bore in on him.

"Right. He was keeping her offa drugs. After she started hangin' with Ritchey, I couldn't hardly get to her. He was a gambler. Now what I heard was he took off a card game somewhere in the Grove." The pimp paused while a doughty waitress freshened his coffee.

"Took it off? You mean he cleaned them out?" Ritchey was lousy at cards, of course.

"No, no. What I heard from Mercy, see, was that he got cheated, or thought so. Left the game and came back an hour later and jacked all of 'em. Dude was pissed off. Had heart. Fearless little motherfucker, know what I'm saying?"

"Is that why he got killed?" I knew what he was saying, about Ritchey, anyway.

"Had to be."

"Where was the card game?"

"The old Lions Lodge in the Grove."

"If you were looking for Mercy, where would you go." I looked across the table at Bones. He was quiet.

"Don' never, please man...they'll kill me..." He looked serious.

"Spill, asshole."

I had my pen ready. Bones described a Salvadoran cafe in a blue painted store front on the west side of Westlake Park. I promised

him I wouldn't give him up. We left the diner
and headed up the freeway. Rush hour being
what it is, I exited the freeway in East L.A.
and proceeded over surface streets to the
Grove. A maroon sedan kept invading a small
place in the rearview mirror. Slack. It had·
to be. Massaging the accelerator, I put
the motor to work. Might as well make life
interesting for him. While he could claim
general law enforcement authority, he was way
out of his jurisdiction.

After I'd run a couple of red lights and
stop signs, Bones caught on to the fact that
I was trying to break surveillance. He
looked over his left shoulder and looked to
me. "What kind of shit you got me into now,
dick?!" I slowed to turn right at a busy
intersection and Bones opened the door.

"Stay in the car, asshole!"

"Fuck that!" He jumped. I must have been
doing forty-five. He rolled, all elbows and
legs. Slack stopped, almost nailing my piss
yellow ex-informant as he came to the curb.
Time for me to ditch both of them.

South on the Long Beach freeway and back
over the Santa Monica Freeway. I got off in
Downtown and made for the 2nd Street Tunnel.
Every car commercial on TV is filmed there.
I put on my four way flashers and got out.
Horns were blaring. It was still rush hour.
Tightening my belt a notch, I climbed under
the car. Sure enough, there was a tracking
sensor stuck on my chassis with magnets.
Like a limpet mine. Whoever had installed
the unit could track my every move without

having to do any detailed pavement work.
Just as a cell phone was useless in the
tunnel, so was the sensor. I pulled it off
and backed the battery screw out, turning it
off. I glided back into traffic just in time
to miss an ass reaming and summons from an
LAPD Motors Unit.

10:30 a.m.

Harry was entertaining the morning crew.
Old geezers like him. He and I coordinated
what was next. Harry had business at the
Repettis and kept his own key for the
Volvo.

Westlake Park beckoned. I was sure that
what Bones had spilled was as close to the
truth about Ritchey's end as I had heard.
Mercy would know more. Harry called to me in
the parking lot as I saddled up. "Watch your
ass, Fitz." He didn't have to say it.

On my way to Westlake Park, I stopped by
Rampart Station, LAPD. The garage was
usually unguarded. Slack's sensor in a gym
bag under my arm, I tossed a passing
uniform a nautical salute. Walking through,
I found a suitable plain wrap narc car,
slid under it, affixed the sensor and
tightened the screw down, turning the unit
on. As deep in the garage as the narc car
was, the unit wouldn't send until the car
was next driven out, probably at night.

Circling the park twice, I spotted a store
front painted baby blue: "Pupusas y Empanadas
de El Salvador." The cafe looked nice
enough. The neighborhood, once grand, had

gone to shit. The park was crawling with hypes and their assorted suppliers as well as recent immigrant entrepreneurs hawking bogus social security cards and driver's licenses. Storefront bodegas emitted a competing cacophony of salsa music and the soccer game. It is another world, growing faster than the one I grew up in.

12:00 p.m.

I docked my short in a nearby garage out of sight of the street and headed back to the cafe. Between the cafe and the garage, I was afforded seven opportunities to load my pockets up with dope. Gangsters kept watch from windows, rooftops, and alleyways as the dealers they'd enlisted in the street trade plied their wares. Grand old apartment buildings and hotels had been converted into modern day tenement barrios.

The cafe was open so I stepped in. Looked like any other Latin owned place in that part of L.A. I took a seat at the counter. An empanada is like a Welsh pasty, only spicy. I ordered two and a glass of beer. I was the only gringo in the place. The majority of the patrons looking like new arrivals. Everyone hauled their things around in plastic grocery bags. I didn't see anyone who even vaguely matched Mercy's horsepower.

The buxom waitress with dyed red hair and jaws working a large wad of chewing gum came over with the tab.

"Is Mercy Peralta around?" I asked.

She contemplated me, jaws going up and down. "I see for you..."

Five minutes passed before a younger Latin male exited the kitchen and approached. He didn't look like he worked in a kitchen. Thin, fair, blue eyes, Levis, golf shirt, snakeskin cowboy boots. "You looking for Mercy?"

"I am." I looked up from the counter.

He looked skeptical. "Come with me."

I followed him through the kitchen and out a back door which I thought would lead to the next street over. Instead, we had stepped into a canyon of concrete, an alley enclosed between two buildings, the exits blocked by other buildings. He pointed up the alley to an iron barred security door in a wall, motioning for me to lead. When we reached the door, he put a gun to my head, told me to look straight ahead. The gun seemed to have come from nowhere. I complied. He called out in Spanish to unseen parties on the other side of the door. My hands were in the air. The door opened. The pressure of the gun barrel to my head told me to move forward.

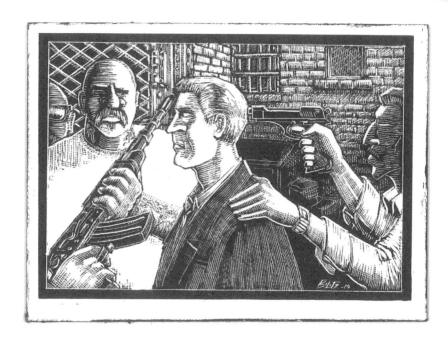

Two other men who looked rougher than the
first awaited me inside. Tattoos, shaved
heads, baggy jeans, a nickelled AK47 slung
over the shoulder of one. It was a crude
foyer, a waiting room. I was placed against
a wall and frisked. No one said a word
when the first drew my revolver from the
holster. Wait I did.

Ten minutes passed and I was led through the
next door and into what appeared to be an
office. There was a Latin man, mid 50s,
seated behind a desk. He looked like a
grocer, but I knew better. There was still a
gun to my head and two others close by.

"Sit down." The older man spoke. "Why'd you
bring that?" He nodded at my gun, sitting on
his desk blotter.

"Comes with the job." He would have
thought me a punk without it. The gunmen
circled in my peripheral vision, guns
leveled.

"You a police?" He seemed doubtful.

"Private eye." He seemed to consider this.
Motioning to me, one of the gang members went
into my back pocket, fishing out my creds.
He looked to Mr. Peralta and said, "For
reals."

"Why do you want to speak with my daughter,
Mr. Fitz?" It sounded like he said "meester
feets." I asked him to take the gun from my
head. He motioned to the younger of the
gunmen. My heart rate started to normalize.

"She and I have a mutual friend who died
recently. I wanted to see if she could tell
me anything about it."

"Who would that be, this "friend"?" He
stroked a whiskered chin.
"Ritchey Renzullo."

"What if I told you that I killed Ritchey?" He
was grinning at me. It was an act.

"I'm not buying it. He was killed by a
punk. You seem like a gentleman, a
businessman to me."

"Okay, Luke Fitz, you're pretty smart. I
didn't kill him, but maybe I should have. For
some reason Mercy liked him. I don't know why.
He was a low life." I said nothing. Mr.
Peralta grinned like a jackal eating a

A CITY OF DEVILS

cherished pet.

I heard the door open again. The gunmen
were gone. There was a raven haired beauty,
green eyes, standing where they had been.
She sat in the chair next to me and wept.
Checking her out, I tried hard not to look
at her like I wanted to look at her. Got to
show some respect. I thought I knew what
Ritchey had seen in her. She told me her
story.

She was sprung on crack when Ritchey met
her. Trading panties for drugs, working the
streets of the Grove, where a pimp like
Bones can be an advantage...protection from
the cops, from the johns, and any pimps with
the impertinence to poach.

Ritchie concealed Mercy from Bones and helped
her kick the drugs, nursing her with malt
liquor and Marlboros. They moved from motel
to motel, always one step ahead of Bones and
Detective Sianez. Ritchey would do his thing
at the horse track during the day while Mercy
laid low, always bringing home enough from
his winnings to keep the rent paid. Ritchey
had plans: to clean up, to leave the Grove,
to settle down. He just had to score a
decent grub stake.

I knew what was next, because I knew Ritchey:
an easy score, not hard work.

Ritchey had planned on robbing the crooked
card game at the Lions Lodge for some time. He
had an accomplice whose name Mercy didn't
know. The accomplice was supposed to alert
Ritchey when there was enough money on the

table to make sticking the place up worth
while. Ritchey knew he'd have to leave the
Grove forever if he did the stickup. It was
the kind of robbery a man might get away with
as the cops would never be called. That is
unless it took place in the Grove.

I asked Mercy when she last saw Ritchey. She
recounted that after the robbery, he had come
back to their room at the Regal Inn. He was
scared. The robbery had gone off without a
hitch. He'd scored big. At least forty
large. He was scared because the haul
included a shit load of cocaine, at least two
keys. An unexpected liability.

Mercy explained that the dealer at the card
game knew Ritchey's accomplice and that was
why the accomplice couldn't do the robbery
himself. Ritchey wanted nothing to do with
the drugs and had an argument with the
accomplice as soon as he got back with the
haul. Mercy heard Ritchey shouting into the
telephone. While the accomplice was on his
way over to collect his share, Ritchey had
sent Mercy across the street to rent another
room. Ritchey never joined her at the Tropic
Palms, and when she saw the coroner's van
with the Sierra Grove Police across the
street the next day, she fled, taking the MTA
Bus to L.A.

"His crimey killed him, I just know
it." She said, referring to he guy
who'd set the robbery up.

"Do you know anything, anything at all about
this guy?" Her father leaned close. He was
at least as curious as I.

"Well, he was a white guy, maybe thirty.
Tall, oh and he was in prison a couple of
times, for like robbery or something.
Ritchey didn't trust him. Said he was a
police informant."

"Where did Ritchey meet him?"

"Maybe in jail, maybe at the horse track...I
never really asked."

That fit like Dick's hatband. Ritchey had
done a few small jolts to county jail. Bad
checks, traffic beefs, shit like that. Living
life low.

"Did you ever meet him?"

"No...I just talked to him on the phone."

"D'you know a girl, a working girl, named
Lisa? Lisa Carpenter."

"Maybe. What's she look like? What track
does she walk?"

I watched Mr. Peralta from the corner of my
eye. Didn't want to get too much into the
prostitution angle lest I offend the nice
man. For offending him or his daughter, I was
sure he would feed me to the wolves standing
by in the next room.

"Tall, red hair, lots of it. Ugly. Claims
she's independent."

Mercy looked up to the ceiling as though for
an answer. Looked down again and replied,

"Never heard of her, but I think I smelled her a couple of times."

"What do you mean?"

"Ritchey's car smelled like cheap ass cologne or perfume a few times. He said he had given a friend a ride. I shined it."

Mr. Peralta handing me my gun was his way of saying good bye. I thanked Mercy for her help, assuring her that I would call her and let her know when I'd made Ritchey's killer. She gave me the number at her father's office. The same guy who'd led back there walked me out. No gun to the head this time. The baldy gangsters eye-fucked me as we walked by. I felt lucky.

6:00 p.m.

I walked into the bar. Shivers was on my stool. He saw me and got up, headed for the john. I picked his beer up, opened the bathroom door, and spotting his pants around his ankles, threw it on top of him in the stall.

When I sat down, Harry said "You're in a good mood." I took a pull on the first beer of the evening. I wanted to get shitty drunk, but felt I couldn't. Too much unfinished business.

After I was half way through my second brew, Harry buttonholed me. "Luke, two guys from LAPD were here this afternoon."

"What'd they want?" I had a little more

beer. Shivers finally exited the john.
He looked natural dowsed with beer, hair
stuck to his scalp.

"You." Harry had that serious 'don"t fuck
with me, Luke' look on his face. He was one
of my dad's friends. I always play it
straight with Harry. "Said they found your
friend Bonais in an alley in East L.A. this
afternoon. He had a bail bond in his pocket
signed by you."

"Dead was he?"

"Oh yeah. Shot in the head and beaten."
Probably Larry Slack. I told the asshole to
stay in my car.

"Misdemeanor homicide. I'll call them tomorrow
Harry. Get me another pop, willya?"

8:55 p.m.

Shivers called for another as Harry poured
my sixth. I unplugged the jukebox and got
on the pay phone. Some people don't like
phone booths. They'd rather yack in public
on a cellphone for all the world to hear.
Some of my finest moments are in the booth
at the Club 120.

Three dimes and some punched numbers got me
Underwood at the Sheriff's Vice Office.

"It's Fitz, in Pasadena. What's shaking?"

"Just the bacon. What can I do for you?"
Underwood had a voice like Darth Vader; deep,

sonorous, big.

"Got any FIs on a chick named Lisa Carpenter? She's a pro works the Grove."

"Did you already run a make on her?" I could hear him going through the shoe box of index cards.

"Yeah, came back negative for name-n-d.o.b."

"Hmmm...here's why Fitz. Lisa Carpenter is an alias of a transvestite named Danny Whiteman. 'bout six feet tall, red hair..."

"No shit? What kind of priors does Mister or uh Missus Whiteman have?"

"Lessee. Robbery....dealing...prostitution, and more of the same. Drew a five year jolt to the joint 'bout ten years back. Came out dressing like a girl."

That explained a lot. Some guys think of prison as penal time. Others think it's Club Med.

"Underwood, can you find out if anyone has nominated Whiteman?" I was asking if Lisa, aka Danny, was a registered informant for any law enforcement agency. It's something narco squads do so they don't wind up poaching each other's informants.

"Yeah, a long time ago. He was enrolled by a member of the old county narcotics task force."

"Who enrolled him?" I was probably asking for too much.

"A detective on loan to the task force..Larry Slack from Sierra Grove P.D." It went without saying that the task force had been shut down because of unproven allegations of corruption on the part of some of the officers. No big surprises.

My next call was to the Grove's dispatch desk. Calling in on that number, they thought I was from their department, not that I would ever tell them such a thing. A radio chattered in the background. I had to hurry because the drunks were getting impatient to plug the jukebox back in. Harry could hold them at bay for only so long. I asked the operator for Slack's location and status. More chatter as she radioed him. He was on a surveillance in the Rampart Division, Los Angeles, but getting ready to suspend for the evening.

Downing my beer, I ambled out to the parking lot, selecting the Volvo for my next bit of work. I took surface streets into the Grove. I pulled the portable scanner out of the glove box and tuned it to the spare frequency the Grove's detectives use.

More chatter as the scanner whirled and buzzed. I tooled down Grove Boulevard to the Tropic Palms Motel. Waiting my turn at the pay telephone at the gas station across the street, I stiffed a call in to the front desk of the motel. The Hindu answered. I asked for Lisa and as he was connecting the call to

Whiteman's room, I hung up.

Motoring around to the back of the parking lot
of the motel, I took up a surveillance
position on the lee side of a van in the lot
and reclined the seat. Room 222 was in
view. Lights dim, dull blue glow of a TV
playing to the drawn curtains.

Stakeouts suck. Hours of crushing boredom,
pissing in a Pepsi bottle, simultaneously
listening to the radio, and trying not to be
lulled into sleep by the traffic on the
scanner. The Volvo can be too comfortable.
Sleeping is not what I had in mind. I was
taking a chance, playing a hunch. There had
to be more than what met the eye.

11:18 p.m.

Radio chatter. Slack's call sign was Papa
9. He radioed dispatch and signed out for
the night. Not three minutes later he
glided into the lot of the Tropic Palms
Motel, backing into the space closest to the
office. He didn't stop at the office. He
knew where he was going. Watching
his progress up the exterior stairs, it
occurred to me that he had forgotten the
champagne and roses. Into Room 222.

I was working things over in my mind. The
Sheriff's Office wouldn't like trying to make
a case on Slack; neither would LAPD. Bad for
their business, not mine. My route would
have to be either the Attorney General or the
DA. My contemplation was cut short by the
arrival of an older Detroit made sedan.
Smoked windows and seats reclined too

far for me to see the driver or his passenger until they got out.

Shaved heads and baggy pants. A gym bag under one gang member's arm. They went to Room 122 and knocked. The door opened to an unlit room. At least three people were in the room directly beneath the one occupied by Slack and Whiteman.

Wednesday, 2:33 a.m.

The blue glow of the television in Room 222 went out. Room 122 was blacked out. No light, no sound. I checked my watch. Should I stay? My question was answered a moment later.

There was a roar like thunder. Someone firing a big gun on full auto. Room 122 was lit by white-orange muzzle flashes. It lasted no more than twenty seconds. The door to Room 122 opened inward. Two gangsters, one with a nickelled AK47, the other with a sawed off shotgun, exited the room and strolled to the sedan. They opened the trunk, wrapped their gear quickly, and closed up. One whistled. The door to Room 122 was still open.

Mercy Peralta trotted out and jumped in the back seat of the sedan.

They pulled out of the lot as though to go to the market. I wasn't long behind them, taking side streets back to Pasadena, sirens wailing in the distance. There was no way I wanted to be anywhere near that blood bath.

The paper the next day reported that an officer of Sierra Grove P.D. was killed in

the line of duty by unknown assailants.
Days passed, and a few more details
emerged. A female informant aiding the
veteran detective was found dead at the
scene. Somehow, Grove Police Department
kept the Sheriff's Office out of the
ensuing investigation. Word on the street
was they weren't pressing the case.

Probably glad to get rid of him. Might
give them a bad name, corruption and all.

That was smart. Behind closed doors, every
cop within gossiping distance was spreading
the word that Slack had been killed with his
boots on...in bed with his "girl." Legends
die hard.

Nothing ever came of the killing of Ritchey
Renzullo, a small time operator chilled in a
small time town. His killers were retired by
a little reverse street justice.

I guess Mercy Peralta had her ways. "Lisa"
was just the name she was looking for. She
was a better poker player than her dead
boyfriend.

About the Author

Photo by Wild Don Lewis

An occasional resident of Pasadena, California, Nils Grevillius is a veteran Private Detective whose interests include fine art, ethnogeography, and cloning thyloscenes.

Made in the USA
Charleston, SC
03 December 2014